"I've often considered it strange that the most intellectual creature ever to walk the earth is destroying its only home. This wonderful story, *When We All Stopped*, helps parents and their children to overcome the disconnect between our clever brains and our loving, compassionate hearts. We must find a way of living in harmony with nature so that both may thrive. I hope this storybook inspires people of all ages to play their part in healing the harm we have inflicted so that together we can create a new future."

Dr. Jane Goodall, DBE
Founder – the Jane Goodall Institute & UN Messenger of Peace

Photography © the Jane Goodall Institute / By Stuart Clarke

TEDEd
Visit Ted-Ed to see an animated version of this story narrated by Dr. Jane Goodall and for more videos on our changing climate.

1% FOR THE PLANET.

6% of the proceeds from the sales of this book goes to support the **Jane Goodall Institute** and their membership with **1% for the Planet**.
onepercentfortheplanet.org

When We All Stopped

Written by Tom Rivett-Carnac   Illustrated by Bee Rivett-Carnac

cottage door press

To Zoë & Arthur, Esmee & Grace

It starts as a whisper,
a word on the air.
It can't quite be heard,
but you know that it's there.

As gentle as sunlight,
as tenacious as hail,
in its route to the heart,
it could not but prevail.

And the people looked up
from their day-to-day tasks,
their day-to-day jobs,
and their day-to-day masks.

They heard or they felt
where the whisper could lead.
And they looked with eyes wide
at what that might mean.

And once they could see it,
they hadn't a chance
to resist the sweet song
of the deep spell it cast.

But the feeling it brought them at first glance was pain,
as they lifted their eyes on the land they had claimed.

Since they saw at last as if raised from a dream ...

They were almost alone on the land and the sea.

For the trees had almost gone and the bees had almost gone and the creatures in their shells by the seas had almost gone.

And the people felt sad as they saw their new Earth,
but they knew this was it ...

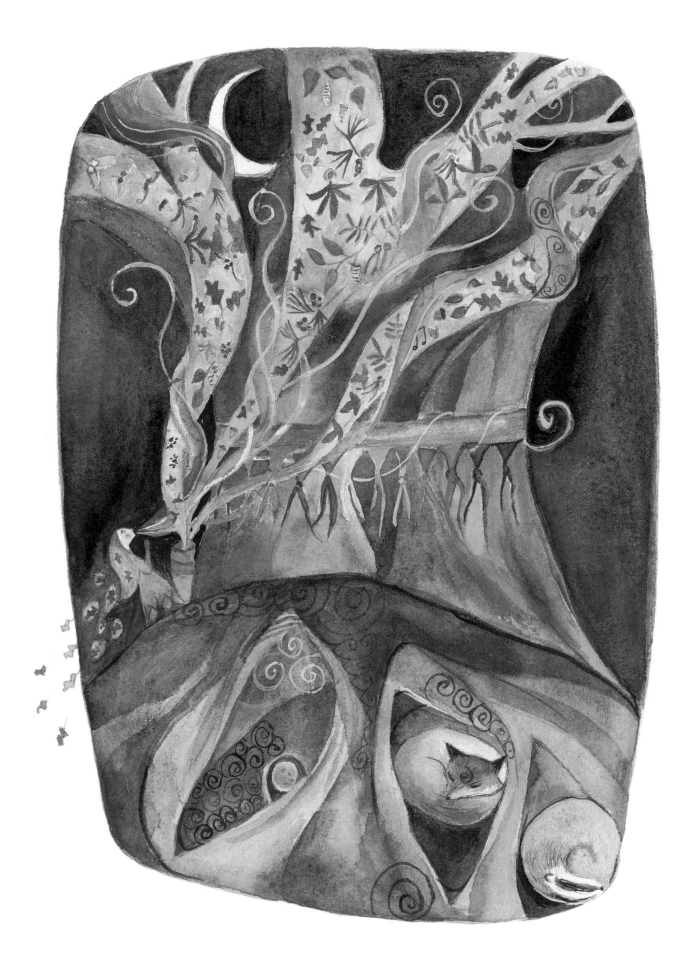

One wild chance for rebirth.

Breaking new ground,
seeds rolling down,
smell of the earth on your hands
and your brow.

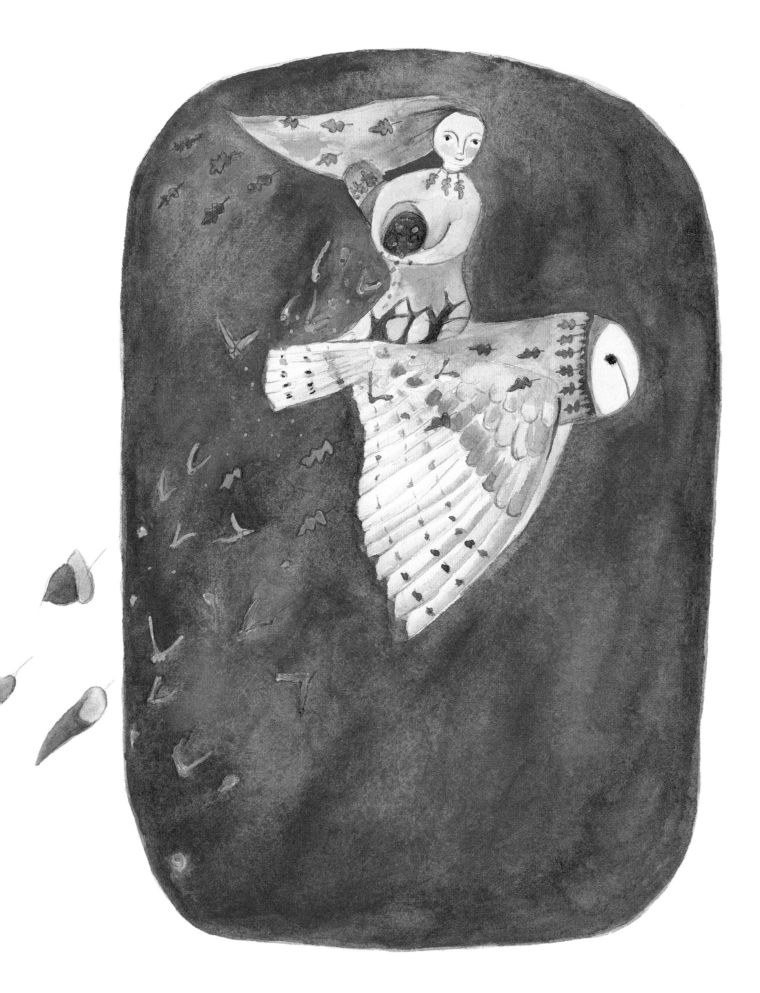

No time for sorrow, we're building tomorrow.
The sound of things growing now keeps us around.

As the wildness grows
and the deep wood grows
and the sense that the future's
come to meet you grows.

There's no chance we can rest,
we must do our best.
This moment can lead us back home,
that's our test.

It starts as a whisper,
a word on the air.
It can't quite be heard,
but you know that it's there.

It then spoke like thunder
until we all moved.
And we could and we did
and it's done ...

She's renewed.

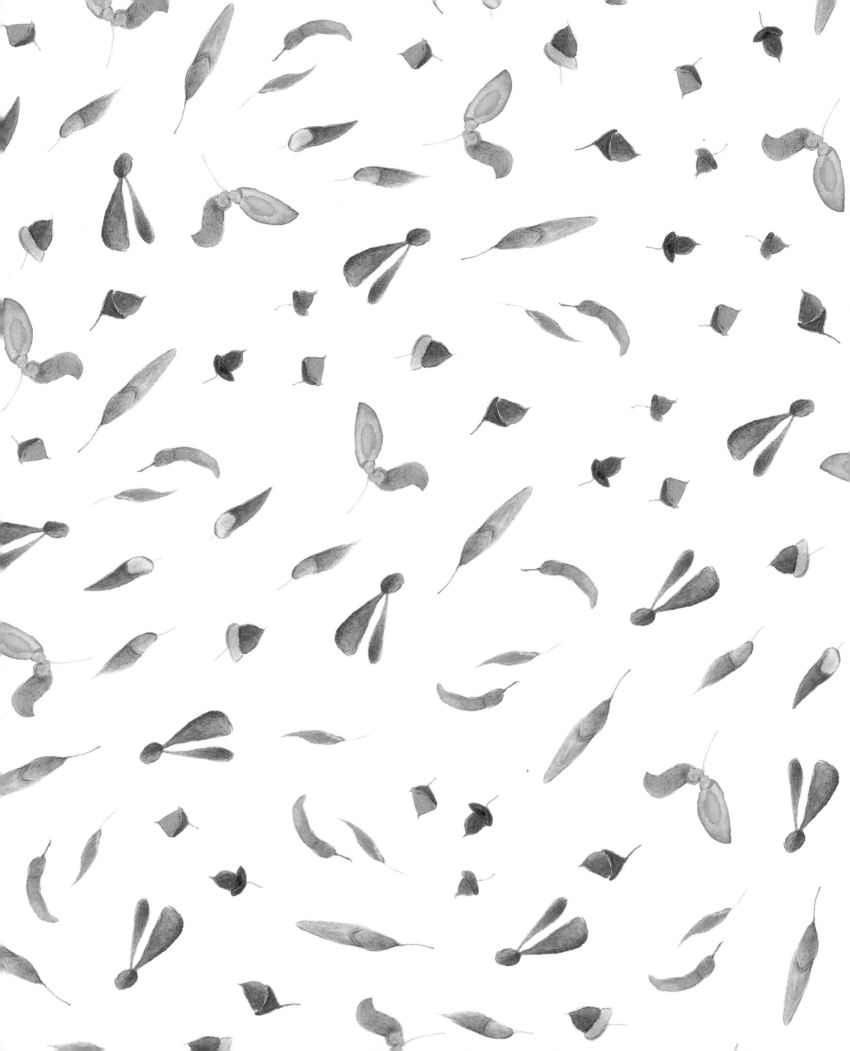